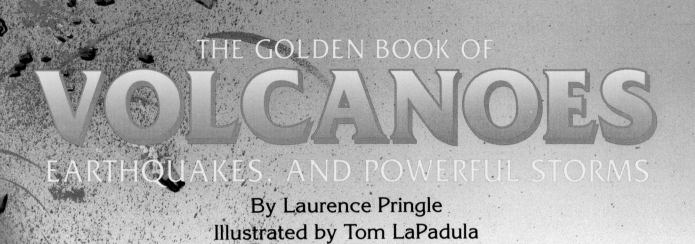

THE GOLDEN BOOK OF
VOLCANOES
EARTHQUAKES, AND POWERFUL STORMS

By Laurence Pringle
Illustrated by Tom LaPadula

Gregory Cavallo, Department of Mineral Sciences,
American Museum of Natural History, Consultant

A GOLDEN BOOK • NEW YORK
Western Publishing Company, Inc., Racine, Wisconsin 53404

Ever-Changing Earth

Our planet, earth, appears to be stable, steady, and unchanging. The sun rises and sets every day, the seasons follow one after the other, and we go about our business, confident in the overall reliability of our environment.

Then suddenly—often without warning—an earthquake levels a city, killing thousands, as it did in Armenia in 1988. A Japanese volcano spews forth lava and threatens to bury a nearby town. A hurricane, like Hugo in 1989, ravages whole Caribbean islands, flattening everything in its path.

Such catastrophic events are dramatic reminders that earth is ever-changing. Since its beginning, powerful forces have been at work steadily altering its surface. Even now these forces are in operation—quietly most times, but occasionally violently—reshaping the earth.

This book is about the great forces of nature that affect all life on earth, and about what human beings have learned from studying them over the years.

In 1988 a devastating earthquake hit Armenia, in Russia. It leveled the city of Leninakan, as well as many mountain villages. Countries from around the world sent help to the Armenians.

In early times people knew nothing about the natural forces that unleashed earthquakes or caused volcanoes to erupt. Often these events were blamed on the anger of the gods. In fact, the word *volcano* comes from the name Vulcan, the Roman god of fire.

In ancient Greece people believed that another god, Atlas, caused earthquakes. According to myth, Atlas balanced the earth on his powerful shoulders. Whenever Atlas shrugged, the earth shook. In other lands people believed that the earth was supported on the back of some giant creature: a great spider, a catfish, an ox, a pig, or, in India, an elephant standing atop a tortoise. When the animal moved, the land shivered and quaked.

Atlas balancing earth on his shoulders

Some 2,300 years ago, the Greek philosopher Aristotle believed that underground winds caused earthquakes and volcanic eruptions. He was wrong, but he was among the first to explain these violent happenings as the result of natural causes. Bit by bit, earth's inhabitants came to understand the great forces of nature. Geology is the science that studies the history of the earth and the natural processes that act upon it. Today, scientists have sensitive devices called seismographs (SIZE mo grafs) that can automatically detect and measure the strength of earthquakes. Hurricanes can be tracked by means of instruments mounted on satellites circling the earth. Echo-sounding techniques can make detailed maps of the ocean floor. Amazing truths about the earth have been uncovered.

A giant catfish carrying earth on its back

9

Our Layered Planet

Scientists now agree that the earth was formed from a fiery ball of dust and gases about 4 1/2 billion years ago.

The heavier elements sank to the core, while the lighter ones rose to the surface. Gases clung to the earth's surface, providing its first atmosphere. Over a long period of time, oceans and soil formed, and plant life, basic to all other life, developed.

Although we live on the earth's crust, lots of questions about what lies beneath our feet remain.

Geologists have so far been able to drill more than 7 miles into the earth's crust. The deeper they go, the hotter it gets. Seven miles down, the earth's crust can be more than 350 degrees Fahrenheit. That's 138 degrees hotter than boiling water! But to reach the center of the earth, you would have to drill 3,950 miles farther!

How Do We Know What's Under the Earth's Crust?

If scientists have drilled only 7 miles into the earth's crust, how can they be sure of what lies below?

The seismograph, the same instrument that tells geologists about earthquakes, also gives them information about the deeper layers of the earth. Geologists now believe that the second layer—called the *mantle*—contains part molten (melted) rock and part solid rock. This mantle is 1,800 miles thick. Beneath it lies earth's third layer—called the *outer core*—which is made up mostly of melted iron and nickel. The *inner core* is believed to be a ball of solid rock some 850 miles thick. Though it may be as hot as the surface of the sun, it is under such great pressure from the layers above that the inner core simply cannot melt.

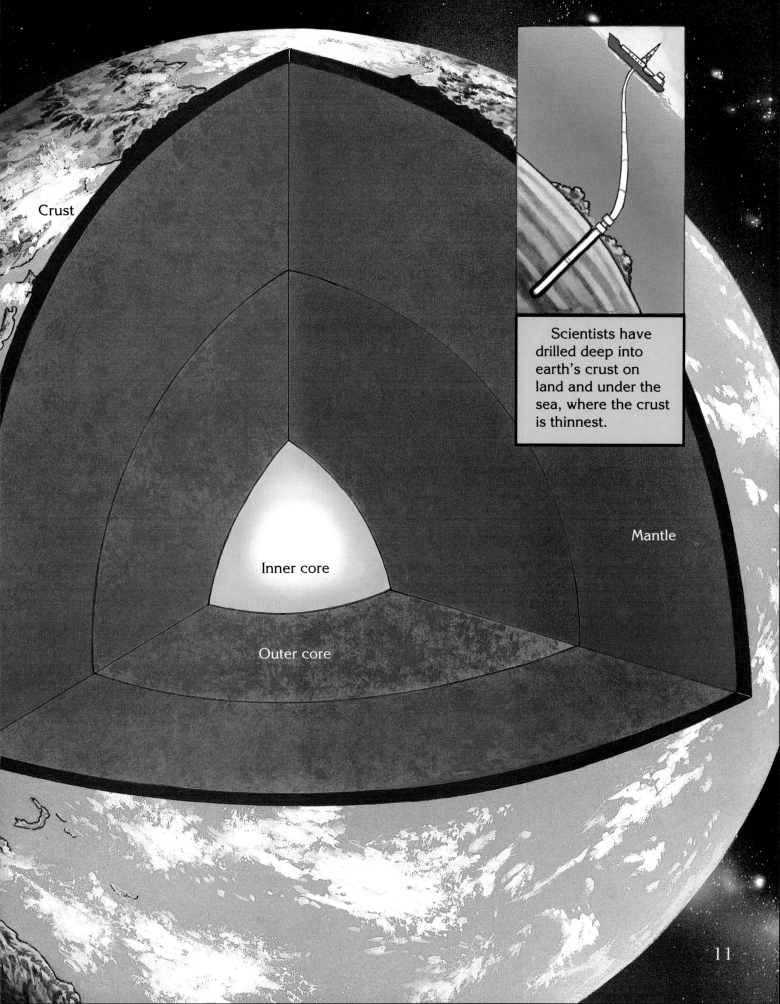

Crust

Mantle

Inner core

Outer core

Scientists have drilled deep into earth's crust on land and under the sea, where the crust is thinnest.

The supercontinent Pangaea
200 million years ago

135 million years ago

A Giant Jigsaw Puzzle

Early in this century a German scientist named Alfred Wegener proposed a theory that all of the earth's continents were once joined together in a single huge continent. He called it Pangaea (Pan JEE a), which means "all lands." He believed that this supercontinent broke up about 180 to 200 million years ago, and that the pieces have been drifting ever since.

Wegener noticed that parts of one continent seemed to fit, like pieces of a jigsaw puzzle, into those of another. Looking at a present-day map, for example, we can see that parts of the east coast of South America seem likely to fit into the west coast of Africa.

As further evidence, Wegener cited the remarkable similarity in rocks and fossils found near the seashores on opposite sides of the Atlantic.

Today, scientists agree that our planet started out as one enormous ocean containing a single mammoth continent. Ever since this great continent split up, earth's land masses have been on the move. By 50 million years from now, some scientists predict, Africa will have split in two.

Slowly, over millions and millions of years, Pangaea began to break up, and parts drifted away from each other.

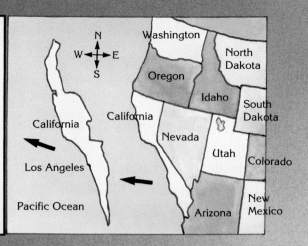

Millions of years from now, Los Angeles, along with much of California, will be heading northwest into the Pacific Ocean, away from the United States. Eventually, this piece of California will collide with Alaska.

65 million years ago

Today

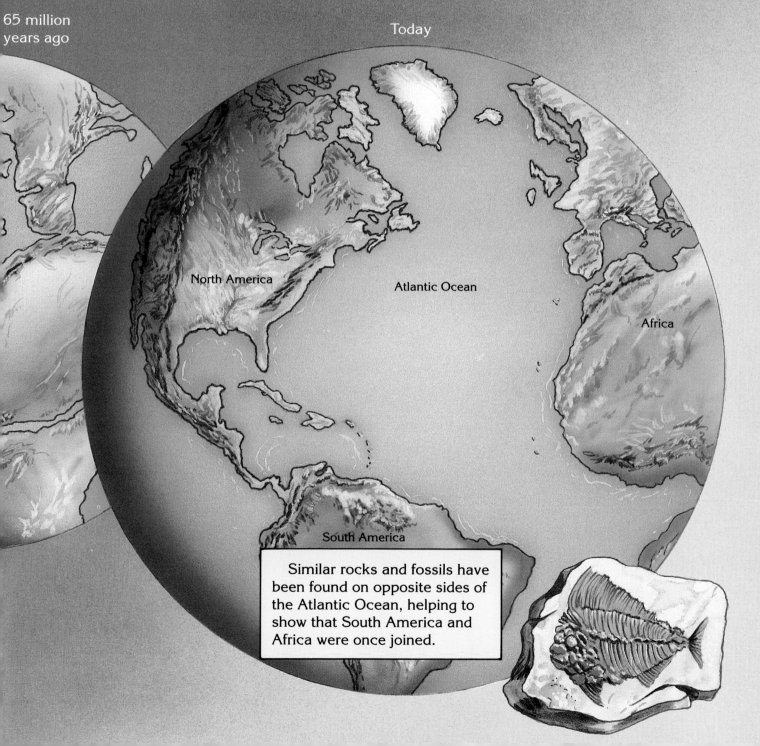

North America

Atlantic Ocean

Africa

South America

Similar rocks and fossils have been found on opposite sides of the Atlantic Ocean, helping to show that South America and Africa were once joined.

Continents on the Move

How do huge continents actually move? Clues to this mystery were found deep in the ocean.

Beginning in the 1950's, advanced instruments enabled geologists to map the ocean floor accurately. As they expected, they discovered vast plains. But they also found a chain of mountains, some 40,000 miles long, that weaves through all the oceans. A deep valley runs through the center of these mountains. It is the longest valley in the longest mountain range on earth.

Scientists now believe that this valley, as well as others found elsewhere on the seafloor, marks the edges of gigantic slabs of rock called plates. Each plate is about 60 miles thick, and is made up of the earth's crust plus the upper solid part of the mantle.

There are about twenty plates on earth. Some are huge. One plate makes up most of the floor of the entire Pacific Ocean, some 6,000 miles wide! A smaller plate carries some Caribbean islands, part of Central America, and the Caribbean Sea.

Like giant rafts, these plates carry continents and ocean basins slowly over the mantle. It is as if the earth's surface were a kind of moving jigsaw puzzle.

The study of these great plates and their movements is called *plate tectonics*. Many questions about earth's plates remain. One of the most intriguing is: What currents or other forces cause the plates to move?

> Valleys on the ocean floor mark the edges of the gigantic slabs of rock called plates.

Continents and oceans ride on the earth's moving plates, some of which are shown here. The plates fit together like an enormous jigsaw puzzle.

North American Plate

Caribbean Plate

Eurasian Plate

Cocos Plate

African Plate

Pacific Plate

Nazca Plate

South American Plate

Antarctic Plate

Sliding, Pushing, Plunging

Melted rock from the mantle is constantly rising up through cracks in the long underwater mountain range. As this molten rock cools, it hardens and becomes new seafloor. This is happening right now in the Atlantic Ocean, which widens an inch or two a year, pushing the United States and Europe farther apart.

But there is a counterforce as well. As the earth's great plates move, some slide past one another. Some, however, push hard against each other. When this happens, the plate of heavier rock pushes slowly under the one whose rocks are lighter in weight. Rocks on land are lighter than those on the seafloor. Each year some seafloor slips under land plates and vanishes into the mantle.

Sometimes two continental plates will collide. About 40 million years ago, the plate carrying India rammed into the plate carrying Asia and Europe. As a result, huge portions of the crust were lifted up to form the mighty Himalaya Mountains.

1. Sometimes two plates ram into each other.

2. When this happens, huge portions of earth's crust may be lifted up to form mountains.

The Himalaya Mountains were formed millions of years ago when the plate carrying India rammed into the Eurasian plate.

17

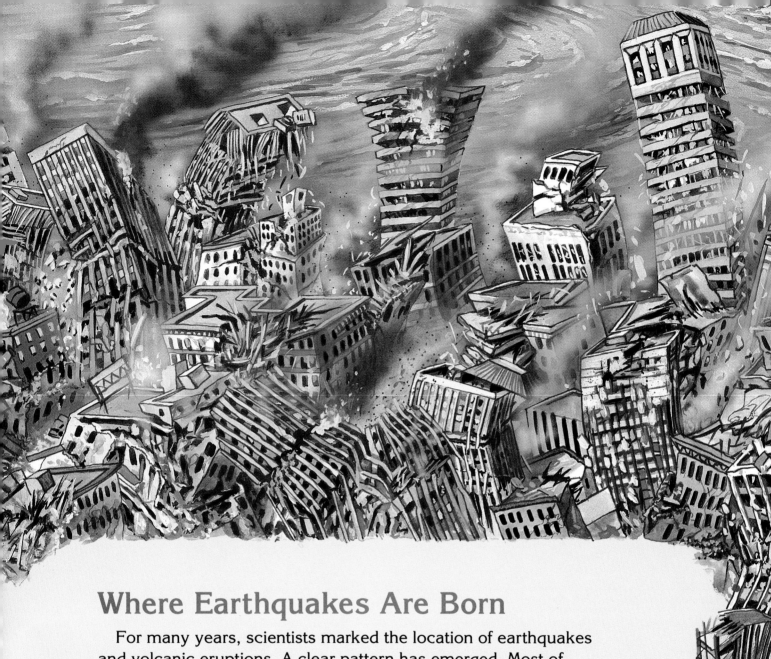

Where Earthquakes Are Born

For many years, scientists marked the location of earthquakes and volcanic eruptions. A clear pattern has emerged. Most of these violent events happen along the boundaries of the plates (the giant "floating rafts") that make up earth's surface.

This is where the rocks of the earth's crust are under greatest stress. They are squeezed and deformed as adjoining plates grind and push against one another.

Although rocks are hard, they can be compressed, bent, and stretched—up to a point. They give way by breaking or shifting position, and releasing stress in the form of vibrations: an earthquake. This seismic (earthquake) energy spreads out in three different kinds of waves detectable by the seismographs that locate and measure an earthquake. The most destructive earthquake waves are called L waves. At the surface, they cause rocks and soil to move up and down. This violent movement can set off landslides, and destroy buildings, bridges, and other structures.

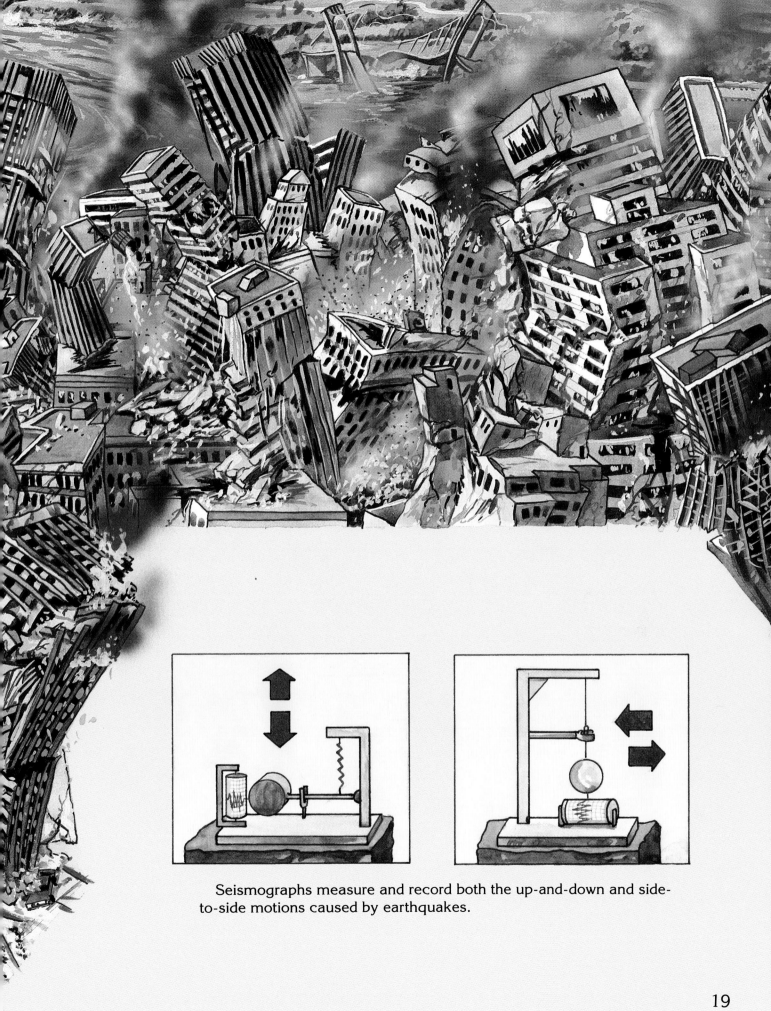

Seismographs measure and record both the up-and-down and side-to-side motions caused by earthquakes.

Cracks in the Crust

Every year approximately a million earthquakes occur, many of them on the ocean floor. Whether minor or major, earthquakes usually occur along cracks in the earth's crust called *faults*. But, wherever they happen, most earthquakes produce tremors so slight people are not even aware of them.

One of the most destructive earthquakes ever recorded took place in Lisbon, Portugal, on November 1, 1755. It was felt by people as far north as Iceland and as far south as Morocco, as far east as Bavaria and as far west as the West Indies.

San Andreas Fault

Faults

One of the biggest, and best–known, faults is the San Andreas Fault that runs through California and into northern Mexico. After the terrible San Francisco earthquake of 1906, scientists found that land on one side of the fault had slipped sharply past land on the other side. Roads that once crossed the fault were no longer connected: the pavement on one side of the fault had been carried up to 21 feet away!

Flying over California, you can actually see the San Andreas Fault. This giant scar, some 650 miles long, clearly marks the border between the Pacific Plate and the North American Plate.

In the fall of 1989 part of the Pacific Plate suddenly slipped about 6 feet past the North American Plate. This happened 11 miles deep in the crust, beneath Loma Prieta, California. The earthquake struck just before a World Series game in San Francisco. The stadium, Candlestick Park, suffered little harm because it was built on rock fill. Structures built on soil or mud were damaged the most. Earthquakes cause these materials to shift more than rocks.

Predicting Earthquakes

In 1975 and 1976 Chinese scientists successfully predicted three earthquakes. One clue that seemed to herald a quake was odd behavior in animals: cows, horses, and pigs racing about for no apparent reason, or snakes slithering out of holes.

In 1975 ninety thousand people were warned to leave the Chinese city of Haicheng just before it was destroyed by a major earthquake. In 1976, however, one of the worst earthquakes of modern times struck Tangshan, China, killing more than two hundred forty thousand people! For every successful prediction, ten false alarms have been issued.

Seismologists, who study earthquakes, have confirmed several warning signs called precursors. While odd animal behavior is one, it is not much help, because it often comes just minutes before an earthquake strikes. More reliable precursors include a rise or drop in the water level of wells, a swarm of small earthquakes, and an increase in hydrogen gas in the soil.

In 1983 seismologists measured a sharp rise of hydrogen near faults in central California. This precursor was soon followed by a strong earthquake near Coalinga.

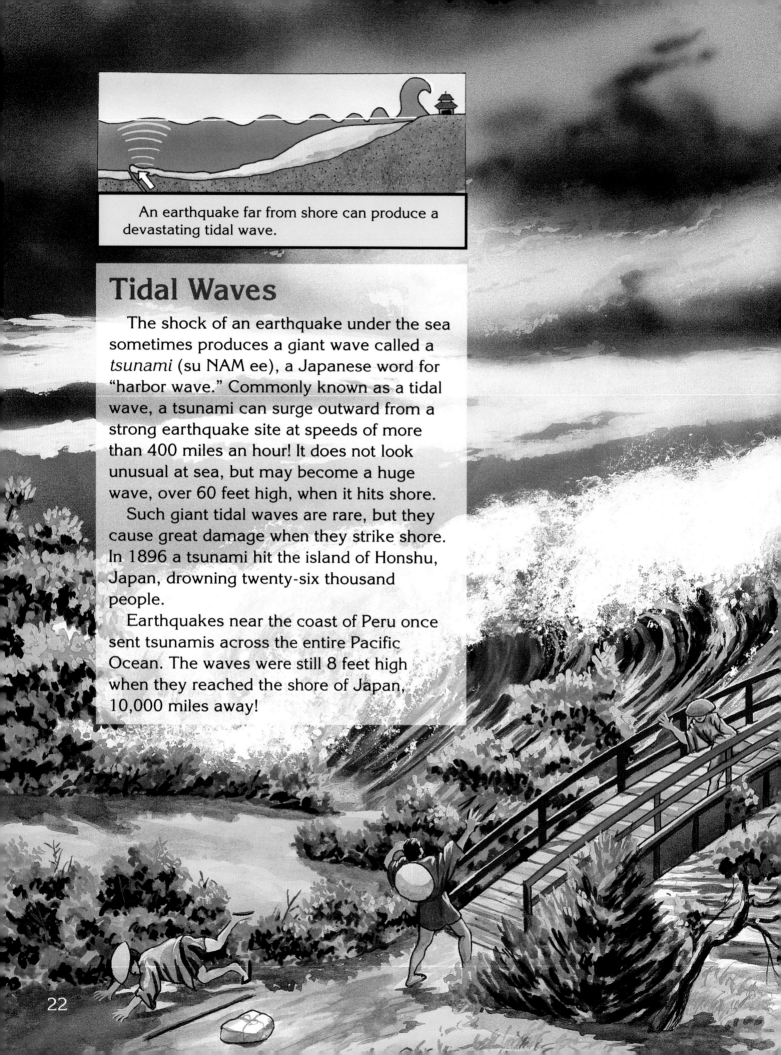

An earthquake far from shore can produce a devastating tidal wave.

Tidal Waves

The shock of an earthquake under the sea sometimes produces a giant wave called a *tsunami* (su NAM ee), a Japanese word for "harbor wave." Commonly known as a tidal wave, a tsunami can surge outward from a strong earthquake site at speeds of more than 400 miles an hour! It does not look unusual at sea, but may become a huge wave, over 60 feet high, when it hits shore.

Such giant tidal waves are rare, but they cause great damage when they strike shore. In 1896 a tsunami hit the island of Honshu, Japan, drowning twenty-six thousand people.

Earthquakes near the coast of Peru once sent tsunamis across the entire Pacific Ocean. The waves were still 8 feet high when they reached the shore of Japan, 10,000 miles away!

Ring of Fire

Some tidal waves arise when volcanoes erupt beneath the ocean. A volcano can form wherever melted rock from the mantle wells up to the earth's surface.

One famous volcano, Parícutin (Pa REE ka teen), began in February 1943 as a small column of smoke arising from a cornfield in southwestern Mexico. By the next day it was a 120-foot-tall cone of cinders. By the end of a year it was a volcano 1,102 feet tall!

Volcanoes do not erupt just anywhere. Nearly all volcanoes are found at or near the edges of the twenty or more great plates in the earth's crust. Here, deep cracks and faults allow melted rock to rise to the surface. Parícutin arose in such a place. So did Mount St. Helens, the volcano that erupted in the state of Washington in 1980.

A world map of some five hundred active volcanoes shows that many of them are located at the edges of the Pacific Plate: in Indonesia, Japan, Alaska, and Central and South America. This pattern is called the Ring of Fire.

Paricutin

Magma and Lava

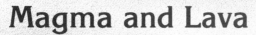

Above ground, volcanoes grow in several shapes. But below ground all volcanoes have two common features: a pool filled with melted rock called *magma*, and a passageway, called the *chimney* or *pipe*, that carries the magma to the surface. Some volcanoes have small pools of magma just a few miles below the surface. But the magma of Italy's Stromboli volcano rises from a pool 155 miles deep!

Magma consists of both melted rock and a mixture of gases. As magma surges to the surface the gases are released and sometimes cause an explosion of melted rock, ash, and other materials.

The melted rock that pours from a volcano is called *lava*. As more lava flows out it gradually builds a cone-shaped hill or mountain. Most lava hardens into rock called *basalt*.

Lava at its hottest can be more than 2,100 degrees Fahrenheit. The hottest lava is yellow in color. The hotter the lava, the faster it flows. Usually it advances slowly, but if it is streaming down a steep volcano's side, lava moves faster than a person can run.

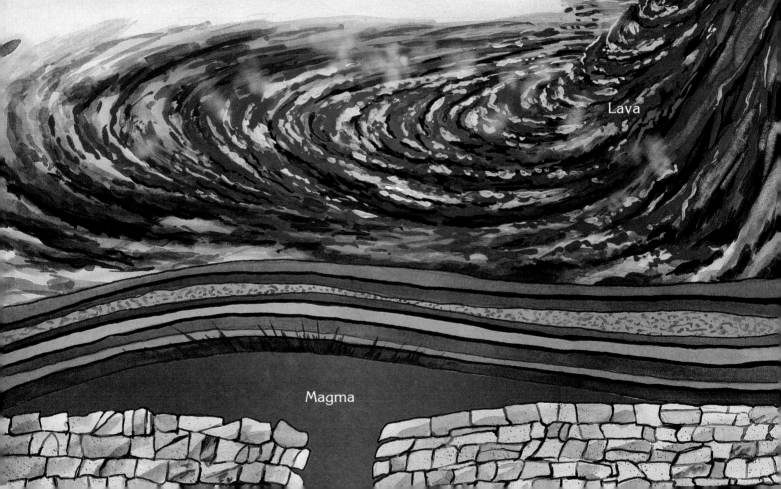

Lava

Magma

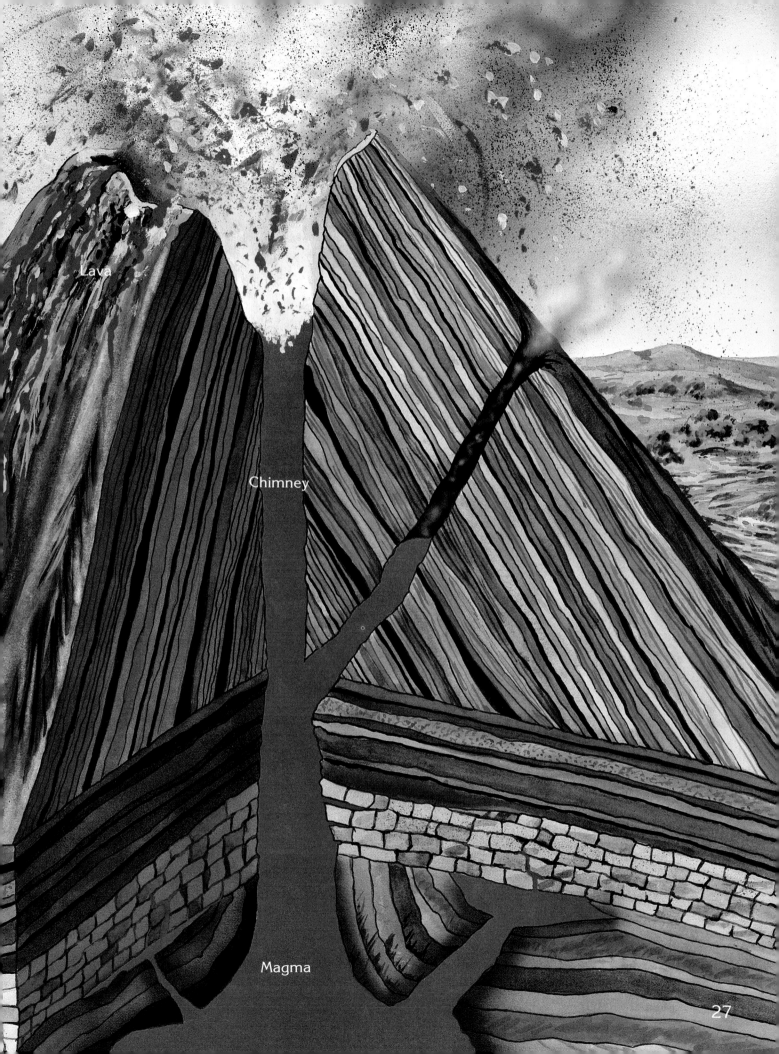

Lava

Chimney

Magma

Island Volcanoes

There are many more volcanoes under the seas than on land. Geologists have discovered some ten thousand volcanoes, each more than 3,000 feet tall, on the floor of the Pacific Ocean. Most are not high enough to break through the water's surface. They are called *seamounts*.

Some undersea volcanoes rise above the surface and become islands. Many volcanic islands are found in the Ring of Fire, along the rim of the Pacific Plate. Others form above a weak point, called a *hot spot*, in an ocean-floor plate. As the seafloor spreads, older volcanoes are slowly carried away from the hot spot, where a new volcano will begin to grow. Over millions of years, a chain of islands may be created.

Maui

Hawaii

Mauna Loa

Under the surface of the sea. The Hawaiian Islands are shown in green.

Loihi, a seamount

Cut-away view of volcanic activity

Magma

28

Molokai

Oahu

Kauai

Niihau

Mauna Loa

Since the ocean is some 17,000 feet deep around Hawaii, countless tons of lava must have poured out of cracks in the Pacific Plate to form the Hawaiian Islands. Mauna Loa (MOE na LOE a), the tallest of three active volcanoes on Big Island, in Hawaii, has a base 70 miles wide. Its height—below and above water—is almost 6 miles, making Mauna Loa taller than Mount Everest. Loihi (LOY hee), a younger seamount growing taller with each eruption, stands 3,000 feet high, under the ocean surface. Thousands of years from now, Loihi will rise above sea level.

Krakatoa: A Volcanic Spectacular

When a volcano's passageway becomes plugged with cooled solid magma, or when it is fed from below with thick, slow-flowing magma, tremendous pressure builds up . Then something has to give, and the top, a side, or the entire volcano explodes. In May 1980 the north slope of Mount St. Helens blew away; the blast knocked trees flat within 12 miles. This mighty volcanic explosion was the most powerful in recent memory, but it is dwarfed by others.

In the spring of 1883 the island volcano Krakatoa, in Indonesia, began spewing ash and water vapor. It hadn't erupted in two hundred years. Then, in late August, it was wracked by explosions for a day and a half.

Some of the blasts were heard as far as 1,250 miles away in Australia. Nearly 5 square miles of ash and other debris reached as high as 30 miles in the sky. Winds spread this volcanic dust around the world, producing sunsets of unusual colors for several years. Dust particles also blocked some sunlight from reaching the earth, causing slightly cooler temperatures (1 to 2 degrees Fahrenheit lower).

The eruption itself, and the earthquakes that accompanied it, launched several tidal waves outward from Krakatoa. The last one rose to 115 feet by the time it struck nearby Java and Sumatra. It erased whole towns, and carried a large steamship 2 miles inland! At least thirty-six thousand people died.

Before eruption

After eruption

Volcanoes usually warn us that they are becoming active. Part of Mount St. Helens bulged more than 300 feet before exploding in 1980.

Powerful Storms

Earthquakes and erupting volcanoes are both dramatic and dangerous. But there are other forces as powerful: the great storms in our planet's atmosphere.

Like the earth's interior, the atmosphere above the earth is also layered. We live at the bottom of the bottom layer, the *troposphere*, which is between 5 and 11 miles deep.

Masses of air in the troposphere are always moving. They are powered by the sun's warmth. When air is heated, it becomes lighter and rises (and colder, heavier air nearer the ground rushes in from surrounding areas to take its place). Meanwhile, the rising warm air expands, cools, and then sinks back to the earth, replacing cold air that has warmed and risen. These constant up-and-down flows of air create the winds that push masses of air along. When masses of air move quickly, a violent storm may result.

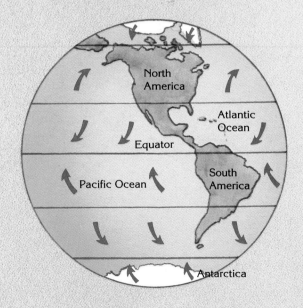

Prevailing wind patterns

Hurricanes

Hurricanes—also called *typhoons, willy-willies,* and *cyclones*—are born late in the summer, over warm tropical ocean waters. A hurricane begins as a giant thunderstorm. Enormous amounts of heat and water vapor rise from the ocean's surface. More air rushes in to replace the moist, rising air, thus pushing it upward even faster. Winds blowing from two directions cause the mass of rising air to begin to spin. The budding hurricane's spin is further increased by the rotation of the earth.

Usually a hurricane moves slowly, but its path is unpredictable. The fast-swirling mass of moist air—perhaps 50 to 250 miles across—has a calm center, called the *eye,* that is about 20 miles wide. This eye is surrounded by towering walls of clouds and raging winds. A tropical storm is called a hurricane when winds reach 75 miles an hour. Hurricane winds of more than 200 miles an hour have been recorded!

Direction of
hurricane

Eye

Direction of
hurricane winds

The torrential rains from hurricanes cause flooding. But a hurricane's greatest threat arises from its effect on waves and tides. Its powerful updrafts lift the ocean's waters, producing high waves and tides as much as 15 feet above normal. As the storm sweeps inland, it not only rips buildings from their foundations, it also washes away beaches and whole areas of islands. Hurricane Hugo in September 1989 caused just such damage on the islands of Jamaica, St. Croix, and Puerto Rico.

Tornadoes

The spinning funnels of air called tornadoes may be tiny when compared with hurricanes, but they are the most violent storms on earth. The United States suffers more tornadoes than any other nation, about 850 every year. Many are born in Texas, Oklahoma, Kansas, and other flat states of the central plains, a region called Tornado Alley.

Tornadoes usually develop in the spring and summer when a mass of cool air clashes with one of warm, moist air. This often produces a severe thunderstorm. Within this storm, columns of fast-rising warm air may begin to spin. About half of these huge updrafts will produce one or more tornadoes. Part of the storm forms a narrow, whirling column of air called a *funnel cloud*. When a funnel cloud touches the ground it is a tornado.

A tornado's appearance may change as it moves. Sucking soil and leaves up from the ground, it becomes dark and sinister. Sucking up water as it passes over a lake, it turns white and is called a *waterspout*.

Generally, tornadoes move at speeds of about 30 miles an hour, but their whirling winds have been measured as spinning at more than 230 miles an hour! A tornado acts like the hose of a giant vacuum cleaner. Its funnel will pick up any object in its path: people, cattle, furniture, trees, roofs of houses, and even small buildings. A tornado's greatest threat, however, comes from the pieces of glass, wood, and metal it flings about at great speeds.

Thunderstorms

Some one hundred thousand thunderstorms rumble and boom across the United States each summer. Powerful updrafts of warm, moist air form clouds that may rise more than 60,000 feet in the sky. Weather scientists call them *cumulonimbus clouds,* or *thunderheads.* A thunderstorm can contain several

of these clouds. Some thunderstorms pass quickly, bringing refreshing showers. A small number are severe and may bring with them rains that cause floods, hailstones that damage crops, and fierce winds that sometimes develop into tornadoes. Since thunder is created by lightning, all lightning storms include thunder.

What Is Lightning?

Inside thunderclouds, electrical charges build up in the tiny particles of water and ice that are tossed around by violent winds. The clouds become charged with electricity—the positive charges accumulating mostly on top and the negative charges mostly at the bottom. These opposite electrical charges are attracted to one another. When they grow strong enough, they connect in the dazzling display we call lightning.

Most lightning strokes leap from one place to another within a cloud, or from one cloud to another. Only about one fifth of lightning bolts reach the ground. This happens when a thin "leader" impulse reaches downward from a thunderhead toward the ground. Then, attracted to the leader, a bolt of electrical energy leaps from the ground or a high object to meet it.

Many lightning bolts that appear to zoom from cloud to ground are actually going from ground to cloud. And what looks like a single flash may be a dozen or more swift strokes that occur in less than a tenth of a second.

What Is Thunder?

Most of the energy of lightning is given off to the air as heat. The air around a lightning bolt's path is heated so rapidly that it expands faster than the speed of sound. As the air breaks through the sound barrier, the result is a noisy shock wave: thunder.

These Great Natural Forces

Volcanoes, earthquakes, and powerful storms can be frightening and disastrous. Fortunately, our understanding of them has grown. Scientists can now give reasonably accurate advance warnings of hurricanes and tornadoes. Someday they may be able to predict earthquakes and volcanic eruptions accurately as well.

Human beings cannot prevent such powerful events, nor should they want to. These great natural forces produce good effects as well as bad. Lava from earthquakes adds new land to our continents and raises new islands from beneath the sea. Lightning plays a role in replenishing nitrogen, which most plants need for growth. They are all part of the continuing process of our ever-changing earth.

Index

A
animal behavior, earthquakes and, 21
Aristotle, 9
Armenia earthquake (1988), 6
Atlantic Ocean, 16
Atlas (Greek god), 8
atmosphere, 32

B
basalt rock, 26

C
Caribbean islands, 6, 35
China earthquakes (1975 and 1976), 21
Coalinga earthquake (1983), 21
continents, movement of, 12-13, 14-15
crust of earth, 10, 11, 20
cumulonimbus clouds, 38-39
cyclones. *see* hurricanes

D
dust from volcanoes, 31

E
earth:
   atmosphere of, 32
   continents, movement of, 12-13, 14-15
   faults in, 20
   layers of, 10, 11
   origin of, 10
   plates of, 14-15, 16, 18
earthquakes, 6
   causes of, 18
   energy waves from, 18
   locations of, 20
   myths about, 8
   prediction of, 21
   scientific study of, 9, 42
   tidal waves and, 22

echo-sounding techniques, 9
electricity, 40

F
faults in earth's crust, 20
funnel clouds, 36

G
geology, 9
Greece, ancient, 8-9

H
Hawaiian Islands, 28-29
Himalaya Mountains, 16
Hurricane Hugo (1989), 6, 35
hurricanes, 6, 34-35
   causes of, 34
   eye of hurricane, 34, 35
   scientific study of, 9
   waves and tides, effect on, 35
   winds of, 34, 35

I
India, 16
Indonesia, 30
inner core of earth, 10, 11
islands, formation of, 28-29

J
Japan, 6

K
Krakatoa volcano, 30-31

L
lava, 26, 43
lightning, 39, 40, 41, 43
Lisbon earthquake (1755), 20
Loihi volcano, 28, 29
Loma Prieta earthquake (1989), 20
L waves, 18